COX

Books should be returned or renewed by the last date
above. Renew by phone **08458 247 200** or online
www.kent.gov.uk/libs

Libraries & Archives

CUSTOMER
SERVICE
EXCELLENCE

The Government Standard

01128\DTP\RN\11.10   LIB 7

To Sophie, another star,
with love K.W.

First published in paperback 2011
First published 2010 by
A & C Black Publishers Ltd
36 Soho Square, London, W1D 3QY

www.acblack.com

Text copyright © 2010 Karen Wallace
Illustrations copyright © 2010 Henning Löhlein

The rights of Karen Wallace and Henning Löhlein to be identified
as the author and illustrator of this work has been asserted by them
in accordance with the Copyrights, Designs and Patents Act 1988.

ISBN 978-1-4081-3053-7

A CIP catalogue for this book is available from the British Library.

Printed and bound in China by C&C Offset Printing Co., Ltd,

Chapter One

Alfie was a meerkat who lived in the desert with his mum and dad, his brothers and sisters, his aunts and uncles and most of his cousins.

Every morning, Alfie's mum woke up before dawn and told her family what to do. The jobs were always the same. First, babysitting, which meant looking after the little meerkats so they didn't run away.

Second, digging, which meant making lots of tunnels to the nest.

And third, watching out for enemies, which meant standing on a big rock trying to spot eagles with sharp beaks or foxes with big teeth.

When she had given everyone a job,
Alfie's mum always said the same thing.
"GO, TEAM! GO!"

And Alfie's dad always said, "AND NO DAYDREAMING!"

He didn't actually *look* at Alfie. But Alfie knew his dad was talking to him. None of his brothers or sisters or cousins had ever had a daydream in their lives!

Chapter Two

One day, everything went wrong.
Alfie forgot about the little meerkats he
was looking after and they all ran away.

He started digging a tunnel to the nest, but the roof fell down on top of his uncle George.

Worst of all, a nasty bird almost ate his sister Fluff because Alfie was daydreaming.

"Alfie!" cried his mum. "We're supposed to be a *team*. What shall I do with you?" Alfie stared at his feet. "I could just stay by the nest and eat insects," he said.

And Alfie's mum said it was the best idea he'd ever had.

The next morning, Alfie sat on a rock, trying to forget about his nasty sisters.

Fluff had called him weird.

Twitch said he was dumb.

And Crumpet laughed and told him he wasn't a *proper* meerkat.

Alfie let out a big sigh.
"Cheer up," said a deep voice. "It can't
be that bad."

An old dog was standing by the rock.
"My name's Bongo," he said.
Bongo pointed to a big black scorpion.
"And this is my friend, Snapper."

Alfie didn't know what to say. The only thing he knew about scorpions was they were good to eat!

Chapter Three

"W-w-what do you want?" spluttered Alfie.
"Nothing." Bongo pricked up his ears.
"We thought you looked sad."
Snapper waggled his claws. "And we want
to be friends."

"F-f-friends?" squeaked Alfie.
Meerkats didn't need friends. They had
each other.

"What would I do with friends?"

"Friends have adventures together,"
said Snapper. "See that sand dune over
there? Something exciting is happening
on the other side!"

Alfie's eyes lit up. He *loved* exciting
things! "Can I have a look?" he asked.
Bongo laughed. "Come with us!"

Alfie followed Bongo and Snapper to the top of the sand dune.

What he saw on the other side made him fall back with a *thump*!

Chapter Four

A herd of monsters were sitting in a circle. They had flat backs and two eyes that stuck out in front. Something that looked like an enormous stick insect was sitting on top of one.

Alfie climbed on top of a thorn bush to get a better look.

Creatures on two legs were running around the monsters. Some were peering into black boxes. Others were talking to furry things on the end of short poles.

Alfie nearly fell out of the thorn bush. One of the creatures was pointing a black box straight at him!

"Bongo!" Alfie squeaked. "What's going on down there?"

"There's only one way to find out!" cried the old dog, and he raced off across the sand with Snapper holding onto his ear.

Two minutes later, they were hiding
behind a rock near the monsters.
"W-w-what are those th-th-things?"
gasped Alfie.

Chapter Five

Bongo whispered in Alfie's ear.
"The monsters are trucks," he explained.
"The stick insects are TV aerials, and the
two-legged creatures are cameramen
who make films."

Alfie blinked. *"What?"*

"Tell him, Snapper," said Bongo.

So Snapper told him about films and television and cameramen.

"Wow," said Alfie. "That's *incredible!*"

"Ssh," growled Bongo. "Here's company."

A thin man and a fat man sat down. "Are you *sure* the meerkat we saw just now is the one you've been watching all week?" asked the thin man.

"Positive," said the fat man. "He's different from the others. Sometimes I even think he's daydreaming!"

The thin man chewed his lip. "And you really want to make a film about him?" "Sure do," said the fat man. "Remember *Super Snake*?"

"That film about the viper?" asked the thin man. "Of course I do – it was brilliant!"

The fat man grinned. "This one's going to be even better."

"OK," said the thin man. "If you're so sure, we'll come back here tomorrow."
"Trust me," said the fat man. "I know a star when I see one."
Alfie's eyes nearly popped out of his head!

Chapter Six

When the men had gone, Bongo turned to Alfie. "Did you hear that?" he cried. "He wants to make *you* a film star!"

"I don't get it," said Alfie. "Why me?"
"Because you're different," said Snapper.
"And you've got what it takes. Now grab
some sleep and we'll meet back here at
dawn. Those cameramen are going to get
the sight of their lives!"

Alfie's sisters were sitting by a rock.
"Had a nice day?" asked Fluff.
"All right for some, sitting around eating
insects," said Twitch.
"*We've* been doing jobs," said Crumpet.

"So what?" said Alfie, with a shrug.
"Tomorrow, *I'm* going to be a film star."

"You've been daydreaming again, dear," said Alfie's mum, from behind the rock.

"No, I haven't," said Alfie. "A man on the other side of that sand dune is going to make a film about me."

Alfie's mum went crazy. "Humans! Into the tunnel!" she barked.
And within seconds, all the meerkats had disappeared!

Chapter Seven

Alfie crept out of the nest while the other meerkats were asleep. It was still dark, but there was enough moonlight for him to find his way to the thorn bush.

"OK," said Bongo. "Now this is the plan... Go back and tell your family that humans are attacking the sand dune."

"That'll get them going!" said Snapper with a chuckle.

Sure enough, as the sun began to rise, Alfie's mum led her family onto the sand dune. They jumped up and down, shook their paws and squeaked their heads off.

It was a meerkat war dance!

When the cameramen were almost at the top of the sand dune, Bongo pushed Alfie forward.

"Do it!" he cried. "This is your chance!"

Chapter Eight

Every bone in Alfie's body was shaking.
"Do *what?*" he wailed.
"Pretend you're a general and this is a battle," hissed Snapper.

"But I'm a meerkat," said Alfie.
"I said *pretend*," Snapper shouted back.
"You're a film star! This is *television*!"

Alfie had no idea what a general was, so he did a few tricks instead. He flipped over backwards …

walked on his hands …

and waved his legs in the air.

44

As the sun rose, his fur shone silver and the sand in the air glittered like diamonds. The cameramen were amazed. Alfie was brilliant!

The first time the meerkats saw *Alfie,*
King of the Desert everyone clapped and
whistled. But Alfie's sisters cheered louder
than anybody.

"You're wonderful," said Alfie's mum, giving him a hug.

"He's the greatest," agreed Bongo.
"A mega film star," added Snapper.

Alfie grinned from ear to ear. For the
first time in his life, he felt *fantastic*.
And, best of all, this wasn't a daydream.
Every single bit of it was true!